A Thief at
WATTLE VALLEY

A CHOOSE YOUR OWN TRACK
ADVENTURE BOOK

AMY CURRAN

A Thief at Wattle Valley
Choose Your Own Track Adventure Book

ISBN: 978-0-6455623-9-2 (Paperback)
ISBN: 978-0-6455623-0-9 (Ebook)

Published in Australia by OUTBACK DESIGN
Taralga, New South Wales, Australia
First published 2022

Original Illustrations: Amy Curran
Cover Photograph: Shelley Webster
Edited by: Denes Illyes, Judy Illyes

National Library of Australia Cataloguing-in-Publication entry information can be found at www.nla.gov.au

Imagine a story so special
that YOU are the star
from the start,
right to the very end.

Enjoy this book
because it's written just for you!

- EMILY -

"You're getting so good, Emily!" Coach Susan said, as Emily walked across the arena towards the gate where Susan stood.

"Good enough to compete in the show?" Emily asked hopefully.

Susan loved to encourage the riders at Wattle Valley, but at the same time she didn't like to make them feel too confident. She would always remind her students that '*you never stop learning*' and '*everyone is good at something different, but that doesn't make them better or worse than you*'.

"Keep practising and riding the way you are, and you just might!" Susan smiled.

"Okay" said Emily with a contented grin, and gave her pony Blossom a pat down her neck.

Blossom was a beautiful pony, bright bay with four white socks and a big white blaze. Emily had only had Blossom for a year, and had been having lessons with Susan at Wattle Valley right from the start.

Emilys parents weren't *horsey* and it took a long time for them to agree to a pony for their horse mad daughter. When they met Susan and discovered Wattle Valley, Emily's dream became possible.

Susan helped Emily and her parents find Blossom, who then came to live at Wattle Valley on agistment, under the guidance of Susan.

Now, a year on, Emily had her sights set firmly on her first ever horse show.

- VICTORIA -

Victoria buckled up the throat latch on her horse Oscar, then grabbed a towel and wiped over her boots. She stood in the breezeway of the stables at Wattle Valley, and admired the beautiful pony in front of her.

Oscar was a striking dapple grey Welsh gelding, around 12.2hh, and was experienced at shows, pony club and dressage. Victoria knew that every other rider at Wattle Valley would give anything for a horse like Oscar, and he was all hers. She beamed with pride as she led him towards the arena for her lesson with Susan.

"Argh" she sighed as she saw Emily walking towards her with her pony. It wasn't that Victoria didn't like Emily, she just found her extremely annoying. There was only two years age difference between them, but to Victoria it felt like much more than that.

Emily was always trying to *help* everyone, but it just held Victoria up and distracted her. Victoria was so focused on improving her riding, every single ride.

"Hi Vicky!" Emily yelled excitedly. "Oscar is looking great today!"

"It's Victoria" she mumbled to herself annoyed. "Hi Emily, lovely to see you" she said louder so Emily could hear.

"Good luck in your lesson!" Emily said as she skipped past her and Oscar.

"I do not need luck you annoying child, I focus and I train, and those who do this, succeed." Victoria muttered.

Victoria could just not relate to Emily and she didn't know why. She continued to walk Oscar to the arena where Susan was waiting.

To continue this book as Emily - turn the page.

To continue this book as Victoria - go to page 15.

"Wow Blossom, you were so good out there today!" you whisper in your ponies ear as you take off the bridle and replace it with a halter and lead. "I know we will be ready for the show I just know it."

Blossom nickered as if in agreeance and you giggle. "I'll take your saddle off and get you some food."

Blossom stood patiently while you prepared the food. Lucerne Chaff, some pellets, and a little bit of oil.

Liam and Anna walked into the stable block chatting away.

"Hey Liam! Hey Anna! Are you both riding today?" you ask.

"Hey Emily!" replied Liam. "Yes I have a lesson in just over an hour, I am just going to get Soloman from the paddock now."

"I am just here to help today" said Anna, "Sonny has been a little hoof sore."

Turn the page.

"Oh no" you reply sadly, not noticing Susans dog Bernie run into the stables towards you.

"Watch that food buck..." started Anna, but it was too late.

You see, Bernie is a very large dog, a Bernese Mountain Dog, and very large dogs need a lot of room without any obstacles.

The force of Bernie launched your bucket into the air, and Blossoms food went everywhere.

Bernie didn't stop though, he kept running right out the other end of the stables.

To follow Bernie out the door go to page 16.

To clean up the mess and get Blossom some new food, go to page 24.

You immediately dismount Blossom and lead her to Victoria to see what has happened, and make sure she is ok.

Susan gets to Victoria at the same time. It seems that somehow she lost her balance and fell.

"Emily, your class is on, you're missing it" Victoria says through painful tears.

"It's ok, you're more important, we are a team, Victoria" you reassure her with a smile.

Susan is impressed. "Go Emily, I have her, go to your class, quickly."

You jump back on Blossom and trot to the ring, just making it in time. You are worried about Victoria, but you concentrate as best you can and are awarded a first place! You can't believe it.

You exit the ring and race back to where Susan and Victoria are.

Go to page 50.

You hang Blossoms rug over her stable door and run to the gear room. Victoria quickly ties up Oscar and follows you.

As you enter you see Anna on the floor clutching her knee, tears running down her face.

"Anna, are you ok?" you ask.

"Anna, what happened?" Victoria chimes.

"I fell, I tripped over my own brush bucket!" Anna cries. "Who would have tipped it over and just left it there like that?"

Victoria crouches down to inspect Anna's knee. "It's a little scraped" she says, "I'll go and get Susan and her first aid box."

You take Victoria's place as she stands and walks out of the gear room. "It'll be ok Anna, Susan will get you fixed up."

You feel terrible thinking about the last conversation you and Anna had.

"I think we need to get to the bottom of all of this mayhem and missing things together," you say. "What do you think Anna?"

"Yes, I think we need to as well" Anna manages a smile.

Susan rushes into the gear room with her first aid kit, and you quickly get out of the way.

"I'll wash Sonny for you ok Anna?," you ask.

"Oh thank you, Emily," Anna replies.

"That's very nice of you, Emily," says Susan.

You realise you best get moving, you have two horses to wash!

Go to page 26.

You tie up Blossom and walk to Oscar's stable.

"Victoria? Are you ok?" you call.

Victoria turns abruptly. "Why do you care? You want me to be *not* ok don't you!" she snaps, tears in her eyes.

"Victoria, I..."

"Stop, leave me alone Emily!"

Confused you walk back to Blossom. '*Wow I won't do that again*', you say to yourself, '*that's the last time I show her I care.*'

At that moment Anna walks into the stables towards you.

To ask Anna to check on Victoria go to page 25.

To continue getting ready to ride Blossom go to page 33.

"Oh man!" you say.

Liam laughs. "We'll help you Em, let's go guys!" he says, and you all make chase after the giant dog.

Bernie leaps and bounds, looking back at all of you every few strides, he is so excited he almost collides with Susan.

"What's going on?" she yells.

"Sorry Susan, my glove!" you laugh as you all jump around to dodge her.

Up ahead, Bernie slows down near the big gum tree beside the orchard. He drops your glove, then continues to walk behind the tree.

Go to page 69.

You ignore the dog and put your legs on, riding Oscar through his spook and just as hoped, Susan is impressed.

"Well done Victoria, great recovery!" Susan praises.

You glance over at Emily, '*she's watching yes!*' you say to yourself. '*You can't ruin me Emily, I will beat you at the show.*'

You watch Emily walk away out of the corner of your eye.

"Well done Victoria, let's end it there for today." Susan says.

You bring Oscar to a walk and near the arena gate.

Susan continues "Cool him down and put him away with a well deserved dinner."

Go to page 66.

You arrive at the arena and say hello to Susan as she holds open the gate for you.

"How's he going, Victoria?" Susan asks, as you lift the reins over Oscar's head and climb aboard.

"Good, I think he could be more forward though, he seems distracted lately" you reply.

"No problems, walk forward into a 20 metre circle and let's see what we can do." Susan replies.

Oscar proceeded through his paces and was working really well. When he did get moving he was such a lovely pony to ride, his canter was like a smooth steady rocking horse.

"Nice Victoria!" Susan praised, "keep your inside leg on, outside leg behind the girth, nice!"

Go to page 39.

You race outside, running after Bernie as fast as you can.

"Bernie, stop!" you yell, as he runs towards the arena where Victoria and Susan are.

"Hey! Bernie!" Susan calls.

Bernie stops, ears pricked slightly, and runs to Susan. She grabs his collar and tells him to sit.

'*Phew*' you sigh, '*that could've been a disaster*'.

Victoria gives you a glaring look. You smile sheepishly and return to the stables where Blossom is waiting patiently. It's a little chilly so you decide to leave her cotton rug that's hanging on the rail outside her stable, and walk to the gear room to find her a warmer one.

Turn the page.

Each horse has its own area of the gear room where their saddle, bridle, saddlecloths, rugs and brushes are. Each horse also has it's own colour, so it is easy to see whose gear is whose if its not put back in the right spot. It is everyone's responsibility to keep the gear room and the stables tidy.

Most of Blossoms gear is pink, her halter and lead, brushes and saddlecloths.

As you pick up a rug, you notice a pink comb in the tub of red grooming gear. *Victoria!* You mutter. You grab the comb.

To confront Victoria go to page 27.

To ignore it and put the comb back in Blossoms tub go to page 31.

You decide to confront Anna and walk outside to find her.

"Anna" you call as you spot her by one of the water troughs.

"Hey Emily, what's up?" she replies.

"Anna, I can't find my pink brush and I had it just before my ride. Have you seen it?" you ask.

"No, sorry I haven't" Anna says, unsure whether she is being accused or asked.

"It's just that I had it only an hour ago, and I asked Liam, and you are the only other person here."

"Wow Emily, are you actually accusing me of taking your brush?" Anna asks annoyed.

You realise you shouldn't have asked Anna like that, and you start to apologise when Bernie bowls past Anna, straight into your legs, knocking you clear over. His giant tail is right in your face as you try to get up and smooth over Anna.

When you finally get up Anna is gone.

You feel terrible. Anna looked genuinely shocked and upset.

'*How could you think it was her?*' You ask yourself. '*But who then?*'

Bernie licks your hand as you brush yourself off and head back to the stables. There's only two more sleeps until the show. You decide to go home for a good nights sleep before a big day tomorrow getting ready.

Go to page 56.

"Emily" you whisper loudly.

Emily turns to you surprised.

"First canter transition, bumpy ground" you continue, "watch Blossom doesn't spook, be prepared."

Emily smiles "Thanks, team mate."

Oscar does a lovely work out, only rushed the down transitions a little. He gets a bit eager when you are nervous and not relaxed.

Emily is next and Blossom works perfectly avoiding the uneven ground. The third rider works out and returns to the line. The Judge calls Emily forward and puts the Champion ribbon around Blossoms neck.

You are mostly happy for her, but can't help feeling a little annoyed that it is because of you she avoided a potential spook at the uneven ground, and that you calmed Blossom down before you even got in the ring as well.

You snap yourself out of it just in time to congratulate Emily.

Turn the page.

The rider who was second to Emily in her class enters the ring and does the same workout in front of the Judge, then comes and positions themselves at the end of the line up.

The Judge calls you forward, and puts the green Reserve Champion ribbon around Oscars neck.

"Congratulations!" you hear Emily say, and you turn and give her a big smile.

Susan rushes in to take a photo of you both together.

"Walk forward Emily" she says, "stand beside each other and smile!"

Emily reaches out and grabs your hand. You give each other a big smile, "Go Team Wattle Valley!"

- THE END -

You decide to unsaddle Oscar and tell Susan. You quickly put him in the stable and rush back to the arena. Liam was about to begin his lesson so you had to be quick.

"Susan!" you yell.

"Yes Victoria, what's wrong?" Susan replied.

"I've had enough of Emily, she took my lead rope and I don't know where it is!" you cry.

"How do you know she took it?" asks Susan.

"It's not there! And she was there!"

"Victoria calm down. That is not proof that Emily took it, or that she even knows where it is. Anything could have happened to it, you can't accuse people of things like that. Now, I need you to calm down and go and finish taking care of Oscar ok?"

Susan was right. You had just left Oscar without his rug on, or without food. You couldn't understand how Emily was able to get to you so badly. You walk back to the stables.

Go to page 70.

'*Argh*' you sigh, and head towards the bucket to clean up the mess. '*Crazy dog*' you mutter.

That dog is always up to mischief. You sweep up the food and place it in the bin. Blossom looks concerned until you return with a fresh bucket, she nickers in appreciation.

As she eats, you put on her cotton rug. As you go to do up the front buckle you notice it's not there. You search the ground, inside the stable, but it is no where to be found.

'*Victoria*' you groan. You are sure Victoria has taken it, no one else would. She is always looking down on you, making you feel like you don't deserve to be at Wattle Valley.

To find Victoria and confront her go to page 27.

To ignore it and use a different rug go to page 17.

"Anna" you call as she nears you.

"Yes Emily?" Anna asks.

"Can you please check on Victoria, I think she is upset."

"Oh, gosh really?" Anna replies. "Yes of course, where is she?"

"In Oscar's stable, I think I could hear her crying." You say, "Thank you."

You listen as Anna walks into Oscar's stable, which is just two down from Blossoms. You try to hear as much as you can, but it is hard to make out all of the words.

'*Green saddleblanket*' you hear Victoria say. '*Destroyed!*'

Oh no, someone has sabotaged her saddlecloth! And you are sure she thinks it was you. You have to find out who did this and prove you are innocent.

Go to page 33.

Blossom is standling patiently when you return with her gear to saddle her up for a last practice ride before the show. You decide on a ride out into the paddock to keep her interested and relaxed before the big day tomorrow.

You trot up the laneway between the paddocks, Blossom is happy and feeling good. You open the end gate into the hill paddock and do some small circles just inside the gate.

'*Look up*' you remind yourself, '*eyes where you are going Emily!*'

You ride off the circle and Blossom pops into a beautiful canter, nicely collected and just the right about of impulsion. You both love a ride in the paddock.

Blossom leaps up the hill, and once at the top you bring her back to a steady walk, ready to head back down.

Go to page 76.

"Victoria, Victoria!" You yell as you run towards the arena.

Victoria brings Oscar to an abrupt halt and glares at you. Susan looks at you astonished.

"Why did you take my things?" you cry.

"Excuse me, Emily?!" Victoria exclaims, clearly shocked at the accusation.

"You are always mocking me, trying to make me feel like a shouldn't be here, and moving my things."

"I have done nothing of the sort!" Victoria says firmly. "I didn't Susan!" she cries as she looks at Susan.

"Emily, calm down," Susan intervenes. "You need to think before you confront someone like this. Did you see Victoria take or touch your things?"

"No, but I know she did!" You cry, and storm off. Bernie follows you back to the stables.

"I hate Victoria!" You say. "I am going to beat her at the horse show."

Go to page 35.

Liam, Emily and Anna are in the stables as you walk in with Oscar.

"Hey guys, can you come over here?" You ask.

"What's up?" Liam asks as they all gather around you.

"All of our sponges are damaged. I just found them while I was in the wash bay." You say.

"What do you mean damaged?" asks Emily.

"Like ripped or cut, I don't know, they're all missing pieces." You explain. "It's time we work together to get to the bottom of this. Find out what happened to the sponges, where our missing things are, and who ruined my saddlecloth."

Everyone agrees. Together you pack the truck to ensure the gear needed for tomorrow is safe, and finish getting the horses ready, as a team.

Go to page 29.

- SHOW DAY -

The sun shines through the early morning fog as one by one, Liam, Victoria, Anna and yourself get delivered to Wattle Valley. Liams mum is taking you all to the show from here, after you have all helped Susan load the horses into the truck.

Bernie bounds through the fog. "No, Bernie, don't jump up I'm clean!" You scream. The rest giggle.

He leaps over to Anna and pulls a glove out of her pocket. "No, Bernie, give it back!" She yells, and tries to snatch it back out of his mouth, but misses.

Bernie runs into the stables, and you all run after him. Before you can catch him, he bolts out the other side, now with your leadrope in his mouth!

Go to page 13.

You shake your head to get rid of those thoughts. '*We are a team*' you remind yourself, and continue to trot forward on the circle.

Oscar is moving beautifully and the Judge calls him in first. Emily next, and the other rider, a boy on a black pony, in to the line up beside Emily.

"I want you to trot out, circle to the left, as you come through the centre canter another circle to the right, back to the middle, simple change and canter to the left, then back to trot towards me and halt." the Judge explains.

You look around the ring as you stand, picturing where your circles and transitions will be. Where your canter transition will be you notice there seems to be an uneven spot in the ground, a horse may spook at this you think.

To quickly warn Emily about the hazard, go to page 20.

To stay quiet and use it to your advantage, go to page 86.

You put the brush in Blossoms tub and take the rug out to the ever patient pony, who is quietly munching through her food.

Bernie comes back into the stables and nudges you from behind. You laugh. "Silly dog" you say affectionately.

Victoria enters the stable block leading Oscar, and ties him up outside his stable. You glance over at her so annoyed that she is messing with your things, you are sure she is sabotaging you.

'*We are going to beat her at the horse show*' you whisper to Blossom as you stroke her neck.

Go to page 35.

You steer Oscar towards Emily and as soon as Blossom sees him she comes back to a walk.

"What's wrong, Emily, are you ok?" You ask.

"I think she is nervous because there are so many horses near her, I can barely control her," Emily says, worried.

"It's ok, walk beside us" You say to Emily.

Blossom is much calmer walking next to Oscar, and you head towards the rings together.

Emily stands next to the ring while you do your class, and Oscar is perfect! You are awarded a first place in a class of a lot of other horses and riders.

"Well done, Victoria!" Emily says as you exit the ring.

"Thank you Emily, it's your turn now, Blossom looks nice and calm."

Go to page 83.

You finish saddling up Blossom and walk out to the arena, through the gate, and stop at the mounting block.

You check your girth is tight enough, put down your stirrups and move the reins over Blossom's head down her neck. You mount and start walking around the arena, gradually gathering your reins to prepare for trot.

You chant to yourself 'squeeze with my legs, think trot, look up, feel the contact' and.... a smooth trot transition! Blossom is working beautifully for you. You know it is your own skills that need improving, Blossom is just so good.

"Hey, Em!" Anna catches you by surprise as she enters the arena with her horse Sonny. "Are we ok to join you?"

"Of course!" You reply.

Go to page 46.

You push Oscar into a big extended trot, between the Judge and Emily. *Flick, flick, flick...* Oscars legs move with so much expression and he certainly gets the Judges attention.

Blossom spooks as you go a little too close to her. Emily loses balance and falls to the hard ground.

"All riders halt!" The Judge yells, and the Steward and Susan rush to Emily who is trying to sit up off the ground. Someone from the crowd grabs Blossom who had started to trot away.

Emily sits up, crying in pain and clutching her arm. An ambulance makes its way across the arena.

Susan storms towards you. "I saw what you did, Victoria, that was horrible! I didn't think you would do something like that for a ribbon. The show is over for you, go and unsaddle your horse."

- THE END -

Liam returns to the stables to saddle up Voltage for his lesson with Susan.

Voltage is a large, bright chestnut gelding with a thin white stripe on his face. He is an exceptional jumper and Liam often goes to jumping events with him. Voltage has mostly green gear.

"Good luck, Liam!" Victoria says as she walks towards him.

"Thanks!" he replies, then turns to you and rolls his eyes, grinning.

"You ok, squirt?" he asks.

"Yeah", you reply "just keep an eye on all of your gear." you say, as you cast your eyes in Victoria's direction.

"Oh?" he says surprised.

Before you can reply Bernie comes up from behind, and headbutts Liam! Liam stumbles and you both laugh.

"Crazy dog!" you both say at the same time.

Turn the page.

- THE WEEK BEFORE THE SHOW -

"Entry forms are here everyone!" Susan yells as she walks into the stables.

Victoria, Liam and Anna all gather around you to hear the details.

"Each of you will have two ridden classes, your rider class in your age group, and your horses class in their breed or height bracket. There will also be a led class. In your rider class the Judge is watching you. Your position, how you deliver your aids and control the horse, and how well you and your horse are presented. In your horses class the Judge is still very much watching you, but also how nicely your horse moves and responds to you, their conformation and again the presentation of both of you."

"I'll schedule some times where we can practice presentation as a group, and we might do a group riding lesson as well if we have time. At the show there will be other riders in the ring with you at the same time.

"Are we all keen?" Susan asks.

"Do cows moo?" Liam says, and everyone laughs.

"Ok, very funny" Susan continues as she sits down on a mounting block with her clipboard. "I will fill these out and drop them off to the Show Secretary tomorrow. You all have one week to be ready. Emily your lesson is 1:00pm tomorrow."

You nod excitedly.

Go to page 74.

Emily had already put Blossom in her stable and hung her pink leadrope across the door. You leave Oscar for a moment and grab the pink lead.

"I'm using yours then!" You say to Emily.

"Fine, whatever." Emily replies, and walks out of the stables.

You tie up Oscar, take off all of his gear and walk it to the tack room to put away. As you walk through the door, Bernie trots out with a feed scoop in his mouth.

You laugh, *silly dog*. You grab some brushes and a rug, and prepare Oscar for his stable and dinner.

Go to page 70.

You were feeling so good, but then suddenly, Susan's dog, Bernie, comes bolting towards the arena!

Oscar jumps sideways, almost unseating you.

"Calm him down, Victoria, woo now, sit deeply, still hands, that's it, back to trot and slow your rising."

You bring Oscar back to a walk just in time to see Emily run out after the giant dog.

"Sorry!" she yells, and continues to run towards you. Oscar snorts tensely as Susan commands Bernie to sit.

To dismount and end your lesson, go to page 65.

To continue riding go to page 14.

You untie Oscar and walk him to the wash bay. There's a bunch of different shampoos in the wash bay, and your favourite for Oscar is the White'n'Bright shampoo. It's purple and makes him look really white, as long as you don't leave it on too long before rinsing out. You've done that before and ended up with a purple pony!

You reach down to pick up your sponge, everyone has their own coloured sponge and you notice a piece missing out of the first sponge you see! You look closer and realise every sponge has missing pieces, every single one!

"What, how?" you wonder. "This is crazy!"

You decide to wash Oscar and then tell the others about the sponges.

Go to page 28.

You can't leave your position and risk missing your class. Victoria didn't see that you had seen her fall, she won't know.

You enter the ring and work out on the circle in front of the Judge. It's a big class, there are at least twelve other riders in the ring with you. The Judge calls in five riders off the circle and you are not chosen. You leave the ring.

Susan stops you as you come out. "Emily, did you see Victoria fall?" She asks in a way that tells you she already knows you did.

"Yes. I'm sorry, I should've helped her" You reply sadly.

"Yes, you should have." Susan says. "That is not the team work that I would have hoped. Go and unsaddle and think about what you have done. The show is over for you."

- THE END -

- THE DAY BEFORE THE SHOW -

It is a beautiful sunny day at Wattle Valley as your mum drives through the gate to drop you off for a big day of preparation before the show tomorrow.

There is so much to be done, a last minute ride, then wash Oscar, plait his mane and tail once he is dry, clean all of your gear and then pack it all into the horse truck.

Susan has a large truck that can carry five horses, with lots of room for saddles and gear as well. The student's parents take them to the events in their own cars, as Bernie rides in the cab of the truck with Susan, and no one else fits if big Bernie is in there!

"Oscar! Come on boy." You call as you walk to get him from the paddock. Susan lets the horses out of their stables each morning, usually early. This lets the horses stretch their legs before their riders arrive.

Oscar nickers and wanders up, resting his head on your chest while you put on his green halter.

Turn the page.

As you walk towards the stables Bernie bolts out of nowhere almost running right into you! *Crazy dog,* you laugh.

Bernie looked like he had something in his mouth as he ran past, but you couldn't quite see what it was and there was no way you would catch him!

You decide to practise for your rider class, and after saddling Oscar and walking to the arena you hop on using the mounting block. You warm him up with an active walk, thinking about the position of your hands. "Look up Victoria" you tell yourself, "ride like you are going to win."

A squeeze of your legs and Oscar lifts up into a trot. "Sit deep, relax" you chant as you sit deeply into a sitting trot.

So many riders dread the sitting trot, but you have practiced it so many times, even without stirrups.

Turn the page.

You do two circles of canter, with a simple walk through change of direction and lead and come back to a walk.

"You're a star, Oscar!" You smile as you lean forward, draping your arms down beside his neck in a hug. You dismount and lead him back to the stables to get him ready for his bath.

As you enter the stables you can hear a sobbing sound coming from the gear room. You tie up Oscar, take his gear off and carry it into the gear room to put it away. As you walk through the door you see Anna on the ground sobbing.

"Anna, whats wrong?" you ask, putting down your gear and kneeling beside her.

"Someone knocked over my things and I tripped over them! Who would do that? I think I have really hurt my knee!" Anna cries.

To get Susan - go to page 49.

To stay and help Anna - go to page 45.

You help Anna up and she cries in pain.

"I don't think it's broken, I am sure it's just grazed, please don't tell anyone, I want to ride tomorrow." Anna begs.

"Well I think you need to take it easy at least for the rest of the day then. I will help you with Sonny, I can wash him, how about you relax here for a bit," You say.

"Ok" Anna nods, "thank you Victoria."

"That's ok, we will get to the bottom of all of this craziness" you reassure her.

You return to Oscar to get him ready for his bath.

Go to page 40.

Anna's horse, Sonny, is a super sweet pony, mischievous and very eye catching. A bright buckskin gelding with a rich black mane and tail, four perfectly even white socks and a beautiful star that drips down his face like a waterfall between his nostrils. He is always the first horse a Judge notices.

You bring Blossom back to a walk alongside Anna.

"So I was just talking to Victoria," Anna says "and she said that someone destroyed her saddle blanket."

"Wow, what?" you ask shocked.

"Yeah, crazy hey! She is so upset." Anna continues.

"I bet she thinks it's me" you say, "I am even more determined to find the culprit now. I have to clear my name."

Go to page 60.

The grounds at Bungendore are full of cars, horse floats and trucks. There are horses and ponies tied to the sides, some in yards and some having a pre-show workout and last minute practice.

Susan parks near a large pine tree towards the edge of the grounds and you jump out of Liam's mum's car to go and help her unload.

"Woohoo! Sonny kept his plaits in!" yells an excited Anna. You all unload the horses and start to take their rugs off to brush them.

Before too long, your led class is on. Susan ties your exhibitor number around your arm. Sometimes the exhibit number is put into a breastplate number holder on the horse but you dont have one of those. Blossom is in the Led Pony mare class, and there is at least six other ponies in the ring with you that you notice.

"You've got this, Em!" Victoria smiles as you walk past. She is waiting for the Led Pony gelding class which is straight after yours.

Go to page 77.

You agree something strange is happening. But hang on, you think, has anything happened to Anna?

To confront Anna - go to page 52.

To continue with Oscar - go to page 61.

"I'll go and get Susan and her First Aid kit." you reassure Anna. "Just stay still until I get back."

You rush off to find Susan, but nearly fall yourself as you exit the room.

"Bernie! Silly dog!" You yell as you regain your balance from his sudden presence.

You find Susan at the clothesline getting in the rugs she has washed for the horses tomorrow.

"Susan! Susan, it's Anna!" you say almost out of breath. "She has fallen in the gear room and she needs you."

Susan runs inside and returns with her First Aid kit, you both run to Anna. When you get back to the gear room Anna is sitting up with her jodphurs pulled up, showing a nasty graze on her knee.

"I'll clean your gear for you, Anna," you say as you leave Susan to treat her knee.

"Thank you, Victoria." Anna replies managing a small smile.

Go to page 40.

Susan stands and gives you a hug. "You deserved that Emily. Not only for your riding but for caring more about Victoria than your class."

"Thank you, Emily," Victoria smiles. "I'm not hurt, well only my pride and my saddle."

The steward calls Victoria's class. You can tell Victoria is upset even though she is not showing it.

To dismount and offer Blossom to Victoria for her rider class - go to page 55.

To go to your next class - go to page 72.

You act like you didn't see Emily and rush to your class without looking back. Oscar becomes unsettled as you enter the ring. He keeps trying to turn back to the warm up area.

You push him forward into a trot and move around the ring with the other riders. It's a large class, you think 11-12 others. Oscar tosses his head and props into a canter.

"No, Oscar! Trot!" You pull him back.

The Judge calls five riders off the circle and you are excused from the ring.

"I should have checked on Emily," You tell yourself.

- THE END -

You decide to confront Anna. As far as you know she is the only one who isn't missing any gear, or has had anything ruined.

You find her wrestling Bernie for the hose. She is laughing but you know you have to get to the bottom of this and interrupt her.

"Anna! Anna!" You call out.

Anna looks up surprised. "Yes, Victoria?"

"Did you ruin my saddlecloth?" You ask firmly.

"Excuse me?" She replies, clearly shocked.

"It's ripped! And Emily is missing a brush, and Liam a hoof pick!" You explain.

Bernie vacates, running towards the main house.

"I cannot believe you!" Anna yells. "How dare you accuse me of such horrible things! Don't talk to me again, Victoria. You're clearly just trying to upset me to get an advantage for the show, well it won't work!"

Anna storms off and you feel horrible.

You go back to the stable to Oscar who is patiently standing waiting for you.

"Oh Oscar, what have I done." You sob.

Go to page 42.

You ignore thoughts of Anna taking your brush, you know her better than that, and walk back to Blossom.

Blossom is standing patiently.

"Sweet girl" you whisper as you brush her. "I don't understand who is taking things around her. It's a complete mystery."

Bernie bowls through the stable block and nudges your leg firmly.

"Hey Bernie" you say "I wish you could talk, maybe you have seen something?" He barks in response, almost as if he does know something.

You laugh and decide to put Blossom away. There are only two more sleeps until the show and tomorrow will be a big day of washing the horses and packing gear.

Go to page 56.

You hop off Blossom and hand the reins to Victoria.

"Hop on, she will look after you. You can't miss your class."
You tell Victoria.

Susan and Victoria are shocked. Through tears Victoria
mounts Blossom and enters the ring. Blossom works
beautifully just like she did for you, just a little more
cautious, like she knew that Victoria was sore. The class
for 13 to 15 years is even bigger than yours, and Victoria is
awarded second!

You and Susan both clap as Victoria leaves the ring with a
huge smile. She jumps off and gives you a great big hug.

"Best friends forever!" She says to you.

"Best friends forever!" You say back.

- THE END -

- THE DAY BEFORE THE SHOW -

The sun is shining down on Wattle Valley as your Dad drops you off to start a big day of preparation.

You've got a long list of jobs which includes one last practice ride, a wash for Blossom, cleaning all of your gear, packing it into the truck and then plaiting Blossoms mane and tail just before you go home.

Susan has a big truck that can carry five horses and it has lots of room for the gear as well. Bernie rides up front with Susan, and the students all get lifts to the show with their parents, some jumping in with others.

You get to work and fetch Blossom ready to saddle her up. Blossom is grazing away and when she sees you she trots up to the gate. Susan lets the horses out into their paddocks early each morning so they can stretch their legs before their riders arrive.

Turn the page.

"Come on, girl, we have a big day" you say as you do up her pink halter.

You walk to towards the stables and nearly have a collision with Bernie who is doing his best cannonball impersonation.

"Gosh that dog is crazy!" you laugh to Blossom. "I am sure he just had something in his mouth though".

You get to the stables, tie up Blossom and start to take off her rug.

Anna walks in, straight past you towards the gear room without saying a word. Victoria comes in next leading Oscar.

Suddenly, you hear a loud scream from the direction of the gear room. It sounds like Anna.

To investigate - go to page 10.

To ignore the sound - go to page 81.

"I am so sorry, Victoria." You say.

"What do you mean Emily?" Victoria asks. "You didn't do this?"

"I know, but I blamed you for my brush missing and I also suspected you, too, Anna. I am so sorry." You reply.

Victoria and Anna come in for a hug. Liam joins in too.

"I think we are all guilty of doubting each other." Victoria says.

"Let's get this cleaned up and get to the show." Anna says as she stands up. "We are a team and teams help each other and make good stuff happen together!"

"We've got this!" Anna and Liam yell together.

Go to page 47.

The grounds at Bungendore are filled with trucks, horse floats and riders, all busy getting ready for the show.

Susan parks near the pine tree on the far side of the ground and Liam's mum pulls up behind. You all clamber out to help unload the horses and get ready.

First up are the led classes, so a quick brush for Oscar, a wipe of his nose and legs, pop his bridle on and he is ready. You fasten your helmet and put on your jacket and gloves. Oscar's show bridle is so pretty, its similar to his usual bridle but has a gorgeous red browband on it.

You watch Emily get awarded second in her class, and congratulate her as she comes out of the ring. You wait for all of the other horses to exit, and in you go, walking nicely beside Oscar trying to get the Judge's attention right away.

Oscar does a lovely big trot across the arena just as the Judge asks, and you are awarded the first place. You quickly duck out and give your ribbon to Emily to hold so you can go back in and work out for Champion Led Pony. The stallion is eventually awarded Champion, and the pretty mare who beat Blossom is Reserve Champion. You are so proud of Oscar though, and so happy with your first place.

Go to page 78.

You bring Blossom to a halt and dismount to walk back to the stables.

Bernie appeared as you exited the arena, he looked like he had something in his mouth but he was running so fast you couldn't quite see.

You get to Blossom's stable and tie her up to unsaddle and groom her. You reach for her body brush and it's not there! You know you just had it before your ride, where could it be? Surely Victoria hasn't sought payback this quickly! Even though you didn't take her saddlecloth.

To look in the gear room - go to page 67.

To look outside - go to page 84.

You stay with Oscar and continue to prepare for your ride, using a spare saddlecloth from the gear room. Thankfully Oscar doesn't know any different and he is calm and happy as you ride out of the arena. You ride him over the trot poles, he really loves those and they make him do a lovely even trot.

Canter transitions are next, trot to canter, both directions, a canter back to trot and smoothly back to a walk.

"You're so perfect, Oscar" you say as you rub his neck and let him cool down in a walk on a loose rein. He stretches down his neck in appreciation.

Go to page 42.

Liam, Anna and Emily rush off to their horses.

"Oh and make time to clean all your gear! Rugs included!" Susan yelled behind them.

You walk to the paddock to fetch Oscar. As you get to the paddock you notice Bernie *helping* Anna fill up the water trough.

"He's really helping you, hey Anna!" You chuckle.

Anna laughs as he runs off with the end of the hose.

"Bernie!" She yells, and you both laugh.

He doesn't get far before the hose runs out of length and he is forced to stop. Anna grabs the hose, which is still running. Oscar trots up curiously to the gate.

Turn the page.

"Never a dull moment!" Laughs Susan. Bernie decides to follow her as she walks to turn off the hose.

You put on Oscar's halter and walk him into the stables, then tie him up ready to saddle. As you enter the gear room, you notice your green saddlecloth has a tear in it! A large, fresh looking tear! It's ruined! You can feel your tears welling so you grab the saddlecloth and run to Oscars stable before anyone sees you.

"Who would do such a thing?" Your mind goes crazy. *"I haven't done anything to anyone!"* You bury your head in Oscars neck and sob. You hear Emily enter the stables and you try and hide behind Oscar. You certainly don't need her to see you cry.

Go to the next page.

Soon Liam enters the stables and you can hear him start talking to Emily. You can't make out what they are saying, but you can make out parts of Emily's words "pink brush" and "missing".

"That's interesting" you think to yourself. *"Someone must have messed with her things, too?"*

You're so distracted with your thoughts that you don't notice Liam enter Oscar's stable.

"Hey, Victoria, are you ok?" Liam asks.

"I don't know, Liam, I am so confused. Someone has ripped my saddlecloth." You reply.

"Oh wow" says a shocked Liam. "What is going on here? I am missing my hoof pick, Emily is missing her pink brush, and now your saddlecloth is ruined?"

Go to page 48.

"Argh! This is pointless!" You say, jumping off Oscar.

"Victoria, wait!" Susan says.

"No, I just cannot stand her! She is out to sabotage me. She wants to win at the show and she knows she is not better than me, so she has to ruin my chances of winning!" You cry.

Susan takes Oscars reins. "Now calm down, Victoria, I am sure that is not it, you are overreacting. She couldn't have made Bernie run out and scare Oscar."

"Maybe not" you mutter to yourself.

"Just focus on yourself and Oscar," Susan continued, "nothing else."

You agree and walk Oscar back to the stables.

Go to the next page.

As you enter the stable block you see Emily returning from the bin. You avoid eye contact and go to tie Oscar up to unsaddle, but his lead rope is missing.

You turn sharply to Emily. "Where is my green leadrope?"

"Umm, I don't know?" Emily says bewildered.

"You do! You took it!" You scream, startling Oscar.

"No I did not, Victoria! I haven't been anywhere near your things, I promise!" replies Emily anxiously.

To tell Susan - go to page 22.

To take Emily's leadrope - go to page 38.

You walk to the gear room hoping to find your pink brush. You look in the other grooming tubs, but there is no pink brush.

Liam enters the gear room. "Hey Emily, what are you looking for?" He asks.

"My pink brush, it's so weird. I had it right before my ride and now it's gone. I left it right here." You explain.

"That is weird" Liam agrees, "My hoof pick is missing too. I had it yesterday and today I can't find it anywhere."

"Wow really? So it's happening to all of us?" You ask.

"Looks like it. Has Anna noticed any of her things go missing or be damaged?"

"I don't think so" you reply.

"Maybe it's Anna," you think to yourself. *"Surely Anna isn't that compeitive that she would sabotage others just to win."*

To confront Anna - go to page 18.

To go back to Blossom - go to page 54.

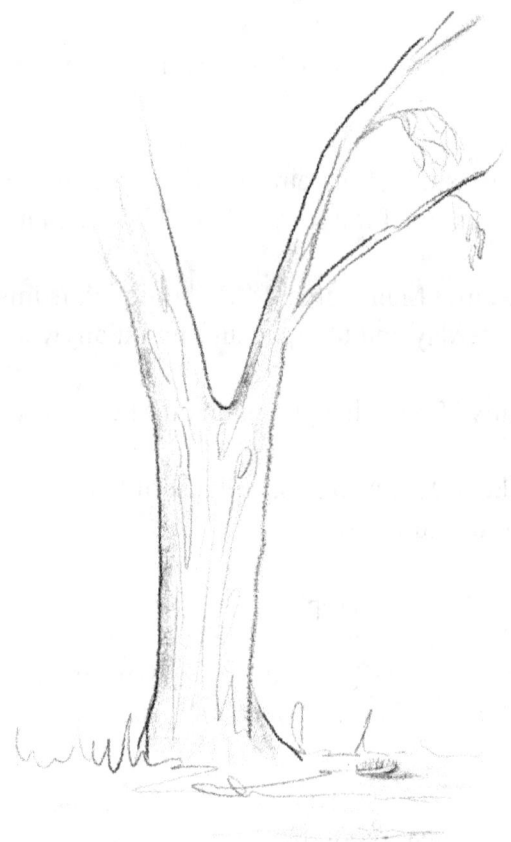

"He dropped it, Emily" Victoria says.

"Hang on, let's keep following him behind that tree." You reply.

You walk around the tree and can't believe your eyes.

"My leadrope!" Says a shocked Victoria.

"My hoof pick!" Liam exclaims.

"Oh wow, there's my comb!" Says Anna.

You notice your brush sitting right there on top of a piece of ripped saddlecloth.

"Bernie!" You all yell at once.

The big crazy dog wags his tail. Oblivious to the fact he is in trouble, any attention is good attention to Bernie!

"What now?" Asks Victoria, still looking shocked.

"Let's clean this mess up." You reply. Together you pick up all of the items and pieces of coloured sponges.

Go to page 58.

- THE WEEK BEFORE THE SHOW -

"Entry forms are here everyone!" Susan yells as she walks into the stables.

Emily, Liam and Anna all gather around you to hear the details.

"Each of you will have two ridden classes, your rider class in your age group, and your horse's class in their breed or height bracket. There will also be a led class. In your rider class the Judge is watching you, your position, how you deliver your aids and control the horse, and how well you and your horse are presented. In your horses class the Judge is still very much watching you, how nicely your horse moves and responds to you, their conformation and again the presentation of both of you and your horse."

"I'll schedule some times where we can practice presentation as a group, and we might do a group riding lesson as well if we have time. At the show there will be other riders in the ring with you at the same time."

"Are we all keen?" Susan asks.

"Do trees have trunks?" Liam says, and everyone laughs.

"Ok, very funny" Susan continues as she sits down on a mounting block with her clipboard. "I will fill these out and drop them off to the Show Secretary tomorrow. You all have one week to be ready. Victoria your lesson is 11:00am tomorrow."

You nod excitedly.

Go to page 62.

You leave Victoria to go to your next class, the Ridden Pony class under 12hh. Another big class with lots of other ponies and riders, and Blossom isn't working as well as she did before. It is almost as if she didn't want to leave Victoria.

You are unplaced in the class and as you are leaving the ring, Blossom is eager to get back to Victoria and Oscar.

You give her a pat and ask her to halt so you can dismount. You feel terrible and know that you should've stayed with Victoria.

- THE END -

You all run after Bernie, he runs all the way to the large gum tree near the orchard and comes to an abrupt stop. The four of you also stop, panting and Bernie starts wagging his giant fluffy tail.

"What is it Bernie?" You say, as you lead the way, walking around behind the tree, the others following closely behind you. "What?!"

"Oh, Bernie" Emily sighs.

"My hoof pick!" Liam exclaims.

"Oh gee!" Says Anna.

A pile of all of the missing stuff. Your lead rope, bits of different coloured sponge and Emily's brush. Liam walks forward and picks up his hoof pick.

Emily turns to you. "I am so sorry, Victoria. I totally blamed you."

"I think we all blamed each other" you reply, "I am really sorry too."

Go to page 88.

Liam, Anna and Victoria rush off to their horses.

"Oh and don't forget to schedule time to clean your gear, rugs included." Susan yelled behind them. "Emily wait!"

"Yes Susan" You reply.

"I want you to concentrate on yourself and Blossom, don't get distracted by anything else."

"Ok," You smile. "I'll do my best to ignore Victoria!"

Susan gives you half a smile, as Bernie bounds in to see whats going on. "And try and ignore this big fellow also!" Susan laughed as she roughed up Bernie, his big thick tail thumping against her legs.

Turn the page.

You walk to Blossom's stable to prepare for a ride. You've decided you will have a practice ride in the arena as there are no other lessons scheduled for today.

Blossom seems eager too and whinnies as you open her door with the halter in your hand. You know that you are so lucky to have such a nice reliable pony like Blossom, she has always looked after you.

"You may not be the biggest or the most valuable horse here, but you are priceless to me Blossom." You say as you do up the halter.

As you lead her through the stable door you notice Victoria in Oscars stable. She has her back turned to you but you can tell something isn't right.

To tie up Blossom and check on Victoria - go to page 12.

To ignore Victoria and saddle up Blossom - go to 33.

You arrive back at the stables and get Blossom ready for her wash. The shampoo and conditioner are kept at the wash bay and you each have your own sponge. Yours is pink, of course.

You walk Blossom into the wash bay, clip her to the tie ups and prepare a bucket of water and shampoo. As you go to pick up her sponge, you notice there is a piece missing out of it! It is half the size!

"No way!" You say loudly. "Who is doing this?!"

You check the other sponges, and are shocked to find all of them missing a piece! Now your mind is really going crazy. You have to get to the bottom of this.

You decide to tell the others after you have washed Blossom and Sonny.

Go to page 79.

Blossom trots out on the lead beautifully and is awarded a second place. "Clever girl, Blossom!" You say after the Judge has tied the bright red ribbon around her neck. You stay just outside the ring and watch Victoria who wins her class with Oscar. He looks so nice clean and is so white.

Victoria goes back in to contest the Champion Pony award, which is eventually awarded to a magnificent chestnut Stallion with four big white stockings called Tango Tom, you have seen him in a magazine before but never in real life. He has the biggest trot you have ever seen.

Victoria comes out of the ring and you walk back to the truck together to saddle up, you are both so pleased with how the show has gone so far.

The first ridden class is your rider class 10 to 12 years. You have practiced so much for this one. After a quick warm up you make your way to the ring. Victoria's rider class is also next, in the ring beside yours, and you can see her walking in a circle waiting for the class to start. Suddenly, as Oscar starts to trot, Victoria falls to the ground! She lands hard on her side. You have to help her! But if you do you will miss your class!

To help Victoria - go to page 9.

To stay so you don't miss your class - go to page 41.

You run back to the truck with Emily to get ready for your ridden classes. Oscar has a black sheepskin numnah that goes under his saddle, just for show days. You really love how good he looks all done up. You use a towel over his legs to remove the dust from the previous class, as well as a quick wipe over your boots and you're good to go.

You head to the warm up area, it's quite crowded so you carefully start to trot, keeping your eyes up to make sure you don't collide with someone else. You hear the announcer call "Class 22". You are class 23 so you bring Oscar back to a walk and head over to line up outside the ring.

As you walk over you notice Emily struggling with Blossom. Something seems to be wrong. You look at the ring and see that class 22 is being judged now. If you leave where you are to go and check on Emily you may miss your class, but she really does seem like she is in trouble and needs help.

To leave and check on Emily - go to page 32.

To pretend you didn't see her so you don't miss your class - go to page 51.

Blossom and Sonny are both washed and in their stables eating their dinner ready to be plaited up. You start with Blossom, and as you begin to comb her mane you hear Liam, Victoria and Anna enter the stables.

"Hey guys!" You call.

"Yes, Emily?" Liam replies as they all gather in front of Blossoms stable.

"We really need to figure out what is going on around here, it turns out the missing gear and the ripped saddlecloth aren't the only things that have happened." You explain. "I just discovered that all of our sponges are missing pieces! All of them!"

"I noticed the sponges, too!" Said Victoria. "It is so strange that it is every single one."

Turn the page.

"It just doesn't make sense. We need to work together to solve this." You say hopefully.

Victoria, Liam and Anna nod in agreeance.

"Let's pack the truck now so we know all of our gear we need tomorrow is safe." You say.

"Good idea," replies Anna. "We all need to help each other now, we are a team! No one is against each other."

"So true!" You reply.

Go to page 85.

You ignore whatever is happening in the gear room. You can't afford to be distracted right now. Instead of riding you decide to do some leading practice with Blossom. One of the classes at the show is a led class.

You lead Blossom to the arena and place a cone where the Judge would be. You stand Blossom near the cone, making sure all of her legs are square and her back legs aren't resting off the ground. You stand at the front of her so the pretend Judge can walk around and inspect her sides and from behind.

Then, you move back to the side and stand beside her shoulder, holding the reins below her chin in your right hand, and the rest of the reins in your left hand.

You walk out a few paces on an angle from the cone, picturing a big triangle shape on the ground. You make a *kiss kiss* sound with your mouth and Blossom pops into a trot beside you as you pick up pace into a slow jog, you turn and trot across in front of the pretend Judge in a bigger extended trot, then back to a slower trot as you turn the corner and head directly back, slowing to a walk, and coming to a halt right in front.

Tturn the page.

"Well done Blossom!" You say as you stroke her neck. You practice a few more times, trying to get a bit bigger trot across the top, then start to walk her back for a bath.

Victoria walks towards you as you near the stables. "Anna fell in the gear room, the poor thing." She says.

"Oh no, how awful, is she ok?" You ask.

"Yeah, Susan is with her now, there is definately something suspicious going on around here."

You nod, "there sure is."

You decide to wash Sonny for Anna. It's the least you can do.

Go to page 76.

Emily and Blossom enter the ring for their class, Blossom is much happier with only a few other horses in there with her, compared to craziness of the warm up area.

Blossom works beautifully and the Judge awards them a first place. You clap excitedly as they exit the ring, Emily is beaming.

"Now you're both in for Champion!" says Susan excitedly, walking towards you both.

"Oh wow, yes we are" says Emily, "I've never ridden in the same class as you, Victoria!"

"It's ok, Emily, we are a team! If you win, I win too, you just get the ribbon" you say, and you both laugh.

Deep down though you do really want that Champion ribbon. You both enter the ring as the Steward calls "those eligible for Champion Ridden Pony Hack!"

Go to page 87.

You walk outside to look for your brush. Maybe I dropped it, you think.

Liam arrives to ride Solomon. "Lost something, Emily?" he asks as he approaches.

"My pink body brush, I had it an hour ago, and now it's missing." You reply.

"That's strange. I am missing my red hoof pick as well, I haven't been able to find it since yesterday." Liam says.

"Well that is super strange, so all of us are missing something, or have had something damaged?" You pause. "Except Anna."

"I doubt Anna wants to win that badly," Liam laughs. "I really don't think she is like that."

"Then who?" You ask.

To confront Anna - go to page 18.

To go back to Blossom - go to page 54.

- SHOW DAY -

Frost sparkles through the paddocks in the early morning sun, as one by one Liam, Victoria, Anna and yourself get dropped off at Wattle Valley to help Susan load the horses. Liam's mum stays as she is taking the four of you to the Show together.

Bernie bounds through the frost. "No, Bernie! Don't jump up on me! I'm clean!" You cry. The rest giggle.

He leaps over to Liam and grabs the sleeve of his jacket. "No Bernie! What are you doing?" Liam yells.

Bernie lets go and runs into the stables, and as you keep watching, straight out the other end with a leadrope in his mouth!

"We need to follow him, right?" You ask, and the others agree and start running after him.

Go to page 73.

You stay quiet, you need the advantage to win, Blossom is working well but you and Oscar want that Champion ribbon.

You ride your workout, carefully avoiding the uneven ground. Oscar feels great, he has such a smooth canter. You come around for your second canter transition and decide to do a flying change to impress the Judge, even though he didn't ask for one.

You are so focused on showing off doing the flying change that you forget about the very spot of uneven ground you thought you could use to your advantage. Just as you ask for the change, Oscar stumbles and you fall forward onto his neck.

You regain your balance just in time to bring him back to a walk and return to the line up. You know you deserved that, and as that beautiful big Champion ribbon is awarded to Emily and placed around Blossom's neck, you can't help but feel very silly.

- THE END -

You let Emily ride into the ring first and Blossom trots off beautifully.

"It's because of us she is so calm" you mutter to Oscar, *"we deserve to win this."*

You squeeze Oscar into a trot, a big expressive trot to get the Judges attention straight away. He is still looking at Emily and Blossom though.

If you cut across the inside of the circle between the Judge and Emily he would have to look at you. But would that be fair to Emily?

To cut across so the Judge looks at you - go to page 34.

To continue riding around on the circle - go to page 30.

You all gather up the items and head back to the stables to help Susan load the horses.

"We are friends, we are a team." You say.

The others nod.

"Let's do this!" Says Anna. "No more doubt, we've got each other."

Emily nods, "I think that silly dog has taught us a valuable lesson."

Everyone laughs in agreeance.

Go to page 59.

ABOUT THE AUTHOR

Amy Curran has written and illustrated over twenty Children's books, including the Tales of Tails series that featured the best selling book *Bobby the Plain-faced Cattle Dog*.

Amy writes and creates her award winning art from her home in rural New South Wales, surrounded by her children, horses, dogs and cats.

Also an accomplished Animal Trainer, Amy trains and prepares dogs, cats and horses for commercial work including Television shows and advertisements, printed catalogues and promotional material for many large companies in Australia and Internationally.

"Every morning you have a choice. You can leave your dreams in your bed, or you can wake up and chase them.
Believe in yourself."
- Amy Curran.